NEW TALES
OF THE
SOUTH PACIFIC

Volume 2

NO PLACE FOR DREAMERS

Graeme Kennedy

NEW TALES OF THE SOUTH PACIFIC
Volume 2: No place for dreamers

About the Author

Graeme Kennedy discovered the South Pacific after moving from his native Australia to New Zealand where he continued his long newspaper career working on mainstream daily and weekly publications and winning a major national journalism award.

Auckland's proximity to the Pacific led him through work and pleasure to the islands he loves and he has visited most of them several times.

In Samoa, Kennedy was honoured with a high chief title in recognition of his writing about the nation and its people.

Kennedy's first book, *New Tales of the South Pacific: Volume 1   Paradise NOT,* is an Amazon best seller in both Kindle and paperback format.

Acknowledgements

I am indebted to my brilliant and hard-working publisher and copy editor Judith Sansweet — and to my always supportive, never complaining wonderful wife Wendy — for their continuing encouragement in bringing this and future volumes to life.

Thanks also to Fairfax Media for permission to use my Aggie Grey 80th birthday interviews, and photograph published in the **Auckland Star,** as A LEGEND. A LIFE.

Colour photo of Aggie Grey
courtesy of Bruce Barton
http://mataipalagi.tripod.com/Samoa/page2.htm

Dedication

All my *New Tales of the South Pacific* books
are dedicated to the indigenous people
of the Polynesian South Pacific.

NEW TALES OF THE SOUTH PACIFIC
Volume 2: No place for dreamers

The eagerly awaited Volume Two of Graeme Kennedy's best-selling *New Tales of the South Pacific* offers another collection of beautifully written short stories based on characters and their triumphant and tragic experiences in a region many believe to be Paradise.

But there is another, gritty side to the Pacific Kennedy has come to know well – a side away from the five-star resorts, where the reality of life makes dreams fragile.

 Beginning with the life story of the Queen of the South Seas, the legendary Aggie Grey, who was thought to have been Michener's model for his outrageous character, Bloody Mary, New Tales of the South Pacific Volume 2 includes stories of black humour, despair in the happiest of Pacific Islands, and the bittersweet ends of two lives of persons who, like Robert Louis Stevenson, go to Samoa to die.

Reminiscent of the great Louis Becke, New Tales of the South Pacific – Volume Two is Kennedy at his best.

NEW TALES OF THE SOUTH PACIFIC

Volume 2: No place for dreamers

CONTENTS

NEW TALES OF THE SOUTH PACIFIC
Volume 2: No place for dreamers

Tale 1 A LEGEND ... A LIFE

I first met Aggie Grey with James Michener at a press conference for the Pulitzer Prize-winning author during a mid-seventies New Zealand book tour.

They had been old friends since the writer first passed through Samoa as a World War II US Navy lieutenant; he described her in his memoirs as "a magnificent woman in her late forties who would become known as the Queen of the South Seas."

A young reporter at the conference asked Michener if Aggie had been the model for the tough old harridan Bloody Mary in his Tales of the South Pacific. He smiled softly and replied, "Oh no. Aggie was much too nice."

BEGINNINGS

Aggie Grey gazes across Apia harbour where dozens of American warships once anchored, and instead of shouts and bawdy songs from US marines hears Samoan girls laughing beneath her window overlooking Beach Road.

The whisky-swilling, girl-chasing young warriors who helped make her famous throughout the Pacific are 30 years gone and American tourists in her hotel bar next door nod over their drinks in the heavy, hot air.

We sip cold Vailima beer and talk as a cooling breeze ruffles the curtains in her apartment and the long Pacific swells smash in white explosions against the reef across the bay.

At 80 years, traces of Aggie's youthful Polynesian beauty and vitality are still evident as she tells the story of romance and determination that brought her forebears to what was in the mid-1800s a remote island

15,000 miles and half a world away from England.

"My grandfather wanted a life of adventure in the South Seas," she says, "so he left Yorkshire and made his home at Levuka in Fiji. He was a chemist and started a small practice there with his two sons.

"About 1895, the American ship Mohican called at Levuka to put a crewman suffering from appendicitis ashore for an operation. One of my grandfather's sons, Willie John Swann, took the crewman's place on the ship and set off to see the world."

Swann didn't get very far.

The Mohican anchored in Apia Bay and with a lawyer friend, Swann rowed ashore to inspect the little German colony. There, the lawyer introduced him to a beautiful young Polynesian woman named Pele (the Hawaiian volcano goddess) and the two fell in love.

Swann stayed in Samoa when the ship left and in a double wedding married Pele as his friend married his Eliza.

"It must have been very strange," Aggie laughs, "because Willie John could not speak a word of Samoan and Pele knew no English – a cousin was the interpreter all through their love business."

After a huge wedding feast and the traditional presentation of fine mats, the newlywed couples moved into an old house on the Apia beachfront. As they had little money, the two brides, Eliza and Pele, sold half their wedding gifts for ten pounds so Willie John could buy medicines and start a pharmacy.

"He was very sad when he learned how they got the money for him," Aggie says, "but it shows that the women were the strongest – and even today women are the backbone – they seem to do the right thing at the right time, and by selling their precious mats, Dad became the first chemist in the islands."

With the business established, Agnes Genevieve Swann was born on Halloween, October 31 1897 and began her struggle through a series of tragedies to the top of Samoan – and Pacific – society.

"I was sometimes very lonely in my childhood," she recalls. "My mother died when I was five and I was not happy at school – we were not very well off and we had to be careful with what we did have.

"As a treat, Dad would give us sixpence for a tin of sardines and we would eat them with some beautiful brown bread from the old baker. My sister Mary and I would sit down under the tamarind trees and I will always remember the taste of the sardine juice soaking into the bread – and even now if I am at a cocktail party you'll find me near the sardines."

And it was one of those brown bread rolls fresh from the local baker that ended Aggie's school days at the age of 12.

"I loved those rolls so much, they were my downfall," she laughs.

"I was eating one, hidden I thought, under the desktop when the nun saw me. She whacked my hand with a bamboo cane, but on the third stroke the tip caught the side of my face, leaving a livid, bright red mark. Then I had to kneel in a corner for half an hour. I was scared stiff of what Dad might do when he found out."

At last, the German nun told Aggie to get up – and the little dark-haired girl went home from school for the last time.

"I packed all my books together and slowly walked out," she says. "I never went back. Dad said nothing when I stayed home, but after four days, he asked, 'Aggie, what about school?

"I pleaded with him to let me stay home and not force me to return. I told him I would cook and wash and help in the shop.

"At last I won the day and he went out and bought three dozen romance and adventure books, a dictionary, pencils and an exercise book. We had lessons at night by the lamp and I came to enjoy the stories – I still read love books and cowboy tales."

Willie John Swann remarried when Aggie was 14, and the family moved to a village near Faleolo to establish a second chemist shop and set up a beachside trading post.

"Sick people from all over the islands would come in canoes to see my father for treatment," she says. "He was highly respected, but we never had a lot of money.

"It was there that I caught typhoid and was very sick for a long time – they didn't think I would make it."

As a blossoming 17-year-old who had inherited her mother's startling good looks, Aggie was taken back to Apia because her father felt she should be near more people.

There, Willie John established a practice in a building adjacent to what is now Aggie's superb hotel on Beach Road.

"I was a pretty little woman then," she says simply, "and I loved to dance – still do. It keeps me young.

"There was a young German clerk in town, Ohle, who was always looking at me and one day he asked me out. He was my first real boyfriend and he took me to my first ball. Dad gave me permission to go – but only if I stayed at the convent that night and Ohle delivered me there by midnight."

The gallant young German complied with the rules – and the couple fell in love.

"Ohle and I were engaged to be married," Aggie says. "There were many mixed marriages then so there was nothing strange about it, but when I was 18 the First World War broke out and that was the end of it."

Aggie recalls Samoa's last German governor, Schultz, telling his men to give themselves up when the New Zealand Forces arrived in Apia Harbour to take possession of the colony.

"They landed just over there," she says, pointing toward the island traders unloading at the docks. "It was all very peaceful – even friendly. There was a six p.m. curfew for the Germans, but everything was so nice. There was no trouble.

"A ship called the Mein came soon afterwards to take the Germans home. They put their businesses in the hands of lawyers, but those who had already married Samoan girls were allowed to stay – the others all left."

With them went Ohle and instead of marriage, Aggie returned to Willie John's chemist shop to spend the war years cleaning mortars and pestles, and probably wondering what life would throw in her path next.

THE BIRTH OF A LEGEND

Aggie Grey pours another cold beer in the hot, still Apia afternoon, taking us back more than half a century to a sad young girl walking alone along the little town's beachfront.

The year is 1915 and she thinks of little else but her husband-to-be, torn from her by the Great War and now somewhere – if he was even still alive – on the other side of the world.

"Then, one day, I was out walking and met a man named Gordon Hay-McKenzie, who told me he had come to Samoa to manage the Union Steamship Company," she says. "I saw him again and our friendship went on until we came to love each other – it took 18 months and we were married when I was 20."

The popular shipping manager and his beautiful young wife lived comfortably in Apia for seven happy years, but they were not without heartbreak.

Their first child, Peggy, later to die of tuberculosis at 21 in New Zealand, was followed by Ian who died at just 20 months, while Pele – named in memory of Aggie's mother – died after her fiftieth birthday. A fourth child, Gordon, moved to New Zealand.

Hay-McKenzie's position demanded regular visits to his New Zealand head office and it was there that seven years into their marriage he, also, died of tuberculosis.

Alone, and with two surviving young children, Aggie turned to her father for help and stayed with him at the Beach Road chemist shop for 18 months. Her period of mourning over, she began mixing again with old friends and through them met young shipping businessman, Charles Grey.

"He came to Samoa from Fiji just for a short visit," she says. "He wasn't going to stay, but he met me – and he did."

At 29, Aggie married Grey in a simple ceremony in Apia, where she again adopted the role of mother and housewife. With her new partner she had three more children: Maureen, who later settled in Sydney; Edward, who went to Auckland; and Alan, today the family head and manager of his mother's world-famous hotel.

She then enjoyed a period of quiet happiness in a marriage that lasted more than a decade until Grey's business fortunes began to decline and, probably through worry and stress, he became ill.

"He went to New Zealand for hospital treatment, but I couldn't go with him," she says. "He died there of a heart problem and I was so mad – the doctors hadn't told me how serious it was.

"When he died, I had nothing, nothing at all, but I was very proud and no one knew how bad things were. The children and I moved into a

little place in Apia and ate Samoan-style –
pineapples, papaya, bananas, taro and fish.

"I grew vegetables and sold them in the
market, and every morning I walked up into the
hills to catch freshwater shrimps in a net I
made."

There, in the cool green cascades bubbling
through the jungled slopes below Robert Louis
Stevenson's grave overlooking Apia Harbour
and the vast Pacific, Aggie netted the fat,
succulent crustaceans before the township
awoke.

She bundled them in banana leaves and sold
them at the market, getting one shilling for 40
shrimps. "I usually got enough to make four
shillings a morning," she says. "It was enough."

At that time, under New Zealand colonial
control, prohibition was strictly enforced.

"You were allowed to drink only if you were
sick," she laughs, "so a brandy or whisky could
be bought only if a doctor supplied a permit.

"But the Germans who stayed after war broke out – those who had married Samoans – applied to the authorities for a licence to run a club where they could drink. When they got it, I was so mad. I figured that if the Germans who we fought against and beat in the war could get a licence, then so should we Samoans."

The spirited young widow found what she thought would be the perfect place for such a club – through a very strange set of circumstances.

The New Zealand authorities who followed the Germans after the outbreak of the First World War were hardly a success in Samoa. Unskilled in colonial administration and with a sad record at home handling their own indigenous people, they caused great discontent among both Europeans and Samoans.

The Samoans opposed the inept administration, and their pro-independence group, the Mau, began a campaign of civil disobedience. New Zealand sent a force of police to Apia to help control the open defiance of colonial misrule and what the powers in Wellington perceived as a real threat of violence.

They were housed in hastily built weatherboard barracks on Beach Road, and on 28 December 1929 – the day still remembered as Black Saturday – were ordered to a Mau gathering a few blocks away in downtown Apia.

This was to be a peaceful demonstration, but within minutes the police panicked, around a dozen Samoans had been shot dead, and another 50 were wounded.

The police returned to New Zealand while conciliation talks resulted in the colonial authorities relaxing their repressive stance and Samoans gaining greater involvement in the administration of their own country.

Samoa in 1962 became the first South Pacific nation to achieve independence.

With the old police barracks vacant, Aggie believed she had found the perfect place for Samoans to have their own club – "But how could I, with nothing, get it and a licence to sell liquor?" she asks.

"Dad agreed it would make a nice club so I went to the government and asked. They said I couldn't do it. I told them I was desperate.

"The man there said the government wanted the building – I said they had enough and I had nothing. I offered him 35 shillings a month to lease it and he eventually agreed to let me try.

"My next battle was to get the vital liquor permit – and I really worked on them. What won it for me was when I said it would be a club for all veteran Samoans, the ones who'd come back from fighting in the war."

But Aggie was almost disheartened as she began to set up her new business. Inside, the old building was a wreck with holes in the floors and walls, peeling paint, and doors hanging off hinges. She knocked down old benzene boxes for wood to nail over holes on the back porch, used them as seats, and scrubbed the place until it shone.

"Dad gave me a chair – the only one in the club; I still have it today – and two standard kerosene lamps. The government wouldn't put electricity in because I had no money."

Aggie's Cosmopolitan Club opened at last in 1937 with great fanfare on the waterfront. Bottles of beer and shots of whiskey sold for one shilling and sixpence and one shilling and nine pence – Aggie made three pence a bottle profit, enough to cover the rent and steadily improve the basics of what would become the most famous hotel in the South Pacific.

"Things gradually got better," she smiles. "I got real furniture and managed to paint the walls. Then one day a young chap named Fred Fairman came to see me – he'd gone broke in the islands and was as poor as I was.

"Fred asked for a room upstairs but there was nothing really suitable. He didn't mind at all, just started cleaning up here and rebuilding there; so it was really Fred who began getting the place off the ground."

The local Samoan men and girls drank there regularly and the Cosmopolitan Club became a social centre for the growing little port town.

"No one had any money in those days," she says. "What we did have we kept for the bad times – and there were plenty of those."

THE WAR YEARS

On 7 December 1941, the Japanese attacked Pearl Harbour – the United States was in World War II.

The massive American military machine built a fighter base at Faleolo where jet airliners now unload tourists, and Apia Harbour became an important supply base with warships anchored in the bay, and huge, ugly landing craft lumbering ashore to spill out the cargoes of war.

"One day soon after they arrived, I was outside my club watching the men unload on the beach across the road," Aggie says. "It was a terribly hot day and they were carrying gasoline ashore, looking very red and tired.

"I walked slowly across the road to them, tapped a sweating Major on the shoulder and said: 'Sir, I bet you'd like a nice cold beer.'

"He hesitated for a second – he thought Western Samoa was still under prohibition – but then he drawled: 'Lady, lead me to it.'"

That single remark, the first American voice she had heard, was to be repeated untold times to create and build the Aggie Grey legend.

Aggie Grey and Bloody Mary are names long synonymous with all that is wild and wonderful about the South Pacific. Both unforgettable ladies earned their fame over decades of exposure to a public dreaming of an unattainable paradise of swaying palms, beautiful island women and clear lagoons.

Bloody Mary, inspired by a betel-chewing Tonkinese copra plantation worker in the wartime New Hebrides, is immortalised in Michener's classic as a tough and conniving itinerant with little regard for her French employers – or any other form of authority.

Aggie, hostess and confidante to US servicemen at her waterfront Apia bar, became famous throughout the Pacific for her generosity, humour and genuine concern for the young transients bound for the coral battlefields further north.

But while the comparisons and attendant international publicity had done no harm to her splendid Beach Road hotel, she long ago turned her back on her mythical counterpart.

"I do not take it as a compliment when people say I am Bloody Mary," she says in the late afternoon shade under the poolside palms. "I have fought against this for a long time, but still they believe I was her."

While locals supported her little club, it was the Americans based in Samoa or passing through who fostered the legend.

"Those first servicemen who came in, sat on my back porch where it was beautiful and cool, and they stayed drinking until night," she recalls.

"The word spread and more and more officers and youngsters came to my place to drink beer and whiskey – they were lovely people, always very polite and helpful, and never any trouble for me."

For the Americans, the club was an oasis in the uncomfortably hot tropics thousands of miles from home – so they made it their own.

"As soon as they started coming to my place regularly, they wanted meatballs, relish, tomatoes and all the food they were used to in the States," she says. "I told them I didn't know much about that sort of thing so one night a group of them went out to Faleolo air base and came back in the morning with everything needed for a hamburger bar.

"They got primus stoves, a pump, tubing and piping – and a huge slab of steel to be used as a hot-plate. Then those fellows assembled the whole thing and told me they'd be back later for the first of my hamburgers and a whole lot of beer.

"Well, I tried and I tried to cook those little round meatballs and I failed. I was starting to panic as the boys would be coming back soon and I hadn't got one cooked properly.

"Then a flying boat landed in the bay and the pilot rowed ashore and came into my club. He took one look at me and said, 'Lady, I see you're in trouble.'

"He showed me how to cook meatballs — you see, I didn't know they had to be flattened."

Aggie, the hamburgers, the beer and dark-eyed young Samoan girls were dreamed of across the Pacific during those long war years and the Cosmopolitan Club name slowly faded away, defaulting simply to Aggie's.

She talks of the wild night beach parties with American officers, the lonely young marines on their way to war cheered by someone who cared — the impromptu, rowdy nights when the bar rocked with laughter, songs and the shrieks of delighted local girls.

"Sometimes, Americans would come in when they were broke," she smiles. They had no money – the girls took it all, I suppose – but they'd order a hamburger and a beer and ask if they could pay later. I'd say OK, son – and you know, not one owed me a cent at the end of the war.

"I have always believed that we must be kind to other people and that your kindness will be returned 10 times over."

Aggie recalls Michener as one of the young lieutenants who frequented her bar in those days – "He was a very quiet man and I liked him a lot and got to know him quite well, keeping in touch even now.

"I would ask him to come back to Samoa and stay at my hotel and he would promise to come when I had a room with his name on the door. Well, we have just finished building some very luxurious private fales and I have sent away for a plaque with his name on it."

The war left Aggie with a well-established and thriving hotel business – and a US Navy boat to drive around Apia Harbour. Legend has it that the Americans gave her a torpedo-attack PT boat and she used it to take tourists cruising up and down the coast.

"But it was a life-boat, made of tin and it leaked a lot," Aggie laughs. "They needed someone to run a boat from the shore to the big warships anchored out in the bay to get officers to and fro, run messages and handle light supplies.

"They provided a 30ft boat and paid me to run the service. I remember the ships – the Lurline, Whipperwill and Ontario – and the hundreds of trips we made out to them and back. The Americans gave me the boat when they left after the war and we used it for a while until it sprung too many leaks and it rusted away."

– AND BEYOND

International air travel and tourism began to take off as peace returned to the Pacific and Aggie made sure her hotel beds were filled with transiting passengers from the huge flying boats that overnighted offshore from Faleolo on their way to Tahiti and the Cooks.

While most of her family settled in Australia and New Zealand, son Alan gave up an academic career to come home and run Aggie's with his vivacious wife Marina and their children.

Fred Fairman, the itinerant carpenter, never left the Beach Road hotel but continued to repair and build and become a jovial part of the family. He and Aggie were lifelong soul mates – her children, grandchildren and almost everyone else called him Uncle Fred.

After the war ended, the Americans still came to Aggie's – aging package tourists from Michigan and Maine replaced the carousing youngsters on their way to war.

They slept in the hot afternoons, and emerged from air-conditioned rooms in the cooler evenings to drink gin and tonics and watch Aggie dance the graceful siva as she did at every fia-fia island night in the big fale.

I remember my own last evening with Aggie; the sun had gone and it was quiet by the pool as the hotel began to stir in readiness for the night ahead – and Aggie, at 80, explained to me how she could never just sit around and grow old.

"I will always dance," Aggie smiled. "There is nothing the matter with me — and I am determined to keep on going until I drop."

Such is the stuff of which legends are made.

With her family at her side, Aggie Grey died at her hotel in her 91st year on 26 June 1988. She lies on the family property at Afiamalu on the slopes of Mt Vaea near Robert Louis Stevenson's old home, Vailima.

On her gravestone is inscribed the most fitting epitaph for a wonderful lady:

There was grace in her steps,
love in every gesture.

NEW TALES OF THE SOUTH PACIFIC
Volume 2: No place for dreamers

Tale 2 DREAMING OF BOATS

Sione Tupou sat on the seawall along Vuna Rd and dreamed of boats.

He gazed at Nuku'alofa's close offshore islands and imagined the big fish he could catch if he had a boat large enough to take him into the deeper waters beyond the reef – fish he could sell for good money at the Tu'imatamoana market near Queen Salote Wharf to make life better for his wife Mele and young sons Viliami and Paula.

But his irregular job as a semi-skilled carpenter with a major building company paid only around five pa'anga an hour – less than four NZ dollars – and that would not buy a canoe and outboard motor, let alone a properly equipped fishing boat three times its size.

Mele also worked, earning around 100 pa'aga a week in a menial clerical role at the Department of Women's Affairs. Tonga had no social security and the public service was absurdly over-staffed to provide opportunities to earn at least something and augment the basics provided and shared by the wider family.

And there were the remittances – money sent home by family members who had left to work for better wages in the United States, New Zealand and Australia. Remittances had become a vital part of the Tongan economy although they had fallen from an estimated 210 million pa'anga in 2008 to 140 million in 2010 – due, he had been told, to something called the Global Financial Crisis.

The offshore funds were usually spent on special purchases such as a home, car – or a boat – but everyone, it seemed, was now short of money.

Although Sione knew his life as an average hard-working and God-fearing Tongan was pretty easy-going, he wanted to be better than average – a lot better – and a good boat could be the vehicle to achieve his dreams.

Sione had grown up in the Ha'apai group about 100 miles north of Tongatapu on the main island of Lifuka near the main town Pangai.

He loved Lifuka and the group's 50 or so sparkling islets and he loved Mele, his village childhood sweetheart who would become his wife. Sione inherited his father's skill and love for fishing and, with healthy yam and taro gardens, the families never went hungry.

He also loved his Mother Ocean for providing such a bounty so easily caught around the nearby reefs, for allowing the island children to play, frolicking, shouting and laughing for hours in the shallows of the lagoon beaches, and he knew he could never live far from the sea.

Sione ended his primary schooling and began working for a Pangai gang of builders to earn a little money doing basic carpentry with hammer and saw as they put up rudimentary village houses – really little more than shacks – and extensions to public buildings.

He and the roundly attractive Mele married in Pangai when they were both 20, and in 2002, celebrated five years of bliss and two children. But living, even among the shining Ha'apai islands, was not always easy.

The European tourists who flew in for two or three days on their way to the Vava'u group 60 miles further north thought staying at the Sandy Beach Resort or Billy's Place was 'cute' and eating out at the Mariner Cafe and Talahiva Restaurant (specialising in mutton flaps, chicken and curry) an 'exotic and happy adventure' – but they were not faced with living a lifetime in what they saw as a Pacific Paradise; they would soon be back home in their comfortable jobs, homes and communities after their brief glimpse of another world.

Sione and Mele talked for a long time –
about how they could improve their lives and
build a real future for their growing family –
before they made the decision to leave their
little island and move to Tonga's capital,
Nuku'alofa, to seek the opportunities they had
heard abounded there.

Sione was particularly eager to join a tuna
boat, one of the fleet of more than 20 long-
liners based there catching tons of the big fish
exported fresh for big money to major markets
throughout Asia and North America.

He had been told crew could earn around
10,000 pa'anga a year – this was very tempting
in a country where the annual wage was 3000
to 4000 pa'anga. The work was arduous – often
demanding 12-hour shifts to bait, lay and
retrieve 50 miles of line that carried thousands
of hooks.

Boats could be at sea for weeks, but the
rewards were great – and Sione knew and loved
the sea. He was also unafraid of hard work.

After much feasting with their Lifuka families and friends, the little Tupou family group boarded the ferry Pulupaki for the 13-hour run to Nuku'alofa and their new life.

It began badly. The long-line fleet had been shrinking as catches and profits fell rapidly. The industry which landed 2000 tons, worth 15 million pa'anga in 2001 was gone by 2005 — the victim of zealous over-fishing by major nations such as the United States and Japan.

Only one big boat continued to chase the tuna while many others, now rotting and rusting at the Vuna Road wharves, told the same sad story of a small country being economically raped by powerful and aggressive plunderers.

The Pacific had been the tuna's home, hosting more than half the world's yellow fin, big eye and albacore species, but the migratory fish were now being caught far from Tonga and they would never return.

Some local boats had turned to snapper fishing, taking the popular white-fleshed species from the tops and slopes of seamounts 400ft down – but this was an enterprise far different from the deep sea tuna hunts and did not offer the same employment opportunities.

A rain shower approaching from the north began to obscure the little resort island of Fafa, and Sione rose from the seawall to walk slowly home, his broken dreams of a better life and adventure on the ocean following him like a pack of forlorn strays.

Mele comforted him with her woman's confidence and assurance that their family had strength enough to overcome this setback – and she was sure that was all it was. They were Tongan, they were one, and together they would succeed no matter what obstacles life and God placed in their path.

They had moved into the basic but comfortable house owned by Mele's brother Mosese and his wife Talita who happily shared their home with the Ha'apai newcomers. Mosese grew taro, squash, pumpkins and tropical fruit on a piece of family land not far along the coast, while Sione and Mele contributed to living costs from their meagre wages.

The house was typical of the average Tongan family living in and around the city of 50,000 – half of Tonga's population – with board walls, iron roof and neatly clipped lawn studded with palms and bright hibiscus. It shared a busy main road with building supply companies, engineering and transport businesses, schools and many churches.

Mosese, like most Tongans, drove a used Japanese import that cost around 8000 pa'anga, paid mostly by remittances sent from relatives in New Zealand specifically for the purchase.

Due to the high cost of electricity, they had no hot water and cooking was done outside in an earth oven or on an open fire. They did not use supermarkets due to cost, but occasionally visited the Talamahu markets sprawling through two downtown blocks on Salote Road that offered a vast assortment of produce, cheap craftwork and lively local gossip.

With almost no disposable income, social life for most Tongans centred mainly around family and the church with everyone gathering at their houses of worship every Sunday to sing songs of praise in full, strident voices booming and echoing through the palms and out to the reef.

Sione and Mosese did not drink in the better Nuku'alofa bars like Reload, or dine at The Waterfront, instead the occasionally visited kava clubs to sit cross-legged on the floor consuming bowls of the cheap soporific drink brewed from roots of the pepper plant and discussing the day's affairs with their comrades.

Much of the debate had recently returned to the monarchy-dominated rule over the Kingdom of Tonga, a polarising issue which some were indolently happy enough to see continue after more than 1000 years. However, an increasing majority were urging for a true people's democratic government rather than one with a majority made up of "nobles" and others appointed by the Monarch.

They felt true democracy was not coming quickly enough – especially after frustration exploded into violence in 2006 when rioting crowds rampaged and looted through Nuku'alofa and burned down buildings in two blocks of Taufa'ahau Road in the city business district. At least six people were killed in the mayhem.

Sione had stayed at home that day, afraid to go into town, but he later heard every embellished detail at the kava club.

Mosese's home suited their immediate needs – it certainly was not in the same class as some of the mansions with tennis courts and swimming pools behind security fences near the shores of Tongatapu's inland Fanga' Uta lagoon, or the large luxury homes owned by the wealthy and privileged, or those rented by expatriate businesspeople at areas such as Anana and Vuna Road.

But it was a mansion compared with Patangata, the pitiful home for a handful of Tonga's poorest. Most under-privileged families located beside the Tukutonga rubbish land-fill – paradoxically at the eastern end of Vuna Road, sadly demonstrating the wide economic gap on such a small island.

Most Patangata dwellers had no jobs or income but eked out a subsistence living by fishing in the lovely lagoon while the women tried to sell woven craftwork at roadside stalls outside homes with roofs of tin sheeting held in place with lumps of coral and walls which appeared to have once been packing cases.

Front yards were bare earth, muddied and puddled after rain, where dogs, hens, pigs and children ran in packs.

Little more than two miles away, just beyond Taufa'ahau Road where construction gangs were rebuilding offices and shops destroyed in the riots, the Royal Palace stood like a grand English cricket pavilion fronted by an acre or more of turf.

Until recently, it was home for the Oxford University and Sandhurst Military Academy educated King George Tupou V who had moved into a sprawling new mansion on a hill out of town. The palace now housed offices, but remained on tourists' must-visit lists.

Sione knew of all this, but between carpentry jobs he was consumed by his passion to buy, beg or borrow a boat to catch the big fish in the deeper waters beyond the reef and make life better for Mele and the boys. He had little time for politics, economics or the King.

He borrowed Mosese's car to drive around Tongatapu visiting villages in search of a second- or third-hand boat. It had to be a solid and safe vessel, about 20ft long, wide-beamed and with a reliable inboard engine powerful enough to drag him to safety should trouble strike beyond the reef.

He returned home in the late afternoon with nothing but disappointment after talking with fishermen at a dozen coastal villages from Hufangalupe and Oholei to Ha'amalo and 'Emeline. He had inspected a range of boats which were either leaking wrecks or plainly over-priced, barely seaworthy hulks.

Sione could never afford the thousands of pa'anga asked for the few suitable vessels he saw — not on his intermittent carpenter's wage in Tonga — but could he do better in New Zealand?

While most Tongans preferred the simple island lifestyle with its year-round warm weather, lagoons, reefs and plenty of fish and tropical fruit, many others believed they could better themselves with the money and job opportunities they had heard were there for the taking in that rich country to the south.

But it would not be easy – friends at the kava club complained that getting a visa for an extended stay in New Zealand was difficult, particularly for Tongans who over many years had built a reputation for remaining beyond time limits. Whether or not those involved were a minority, the stigma remained long after the well-publicised police dawn raids on Tongan families in their South Auckland homes during the Eighties.

Over-stayers in the past had been a major problem and had spoiled the New Zealand dream for many who hoped to follow them. Samoans, Cook Islanders and Niueans all had closer relationships with Wellington while Tongans remained at the bottom of the Polynesian heap despite the many thousands who now resided there, either by immigration or by birth.

For at least a year, Sione and Mele talked long and seriously about moving to New Zealand to work and earn better money for their futures back in the islands while Viliami and Paula would benefit from some multi-cultural schooling.

It would be a huge disruption to their lives – if it was possible at all – but while Mele shared her husband's goals, the boys saw a wonderful adventure ahead of them in a big city with new friends, experiences and tales to tell when they returned home.

The New Zealand immigration officer at the consulate in Taufa'ahau Road took little time to grant the Tupou family their permits. After all, Sione was known as an honest and hard worker with an impeccable background and, perhaps most important, no police file.

They told family they would be gone "just for a while," and with what money they had farewelled Mosese and Talita at Fua'amotu and boarded the flight south.

Auckland International Airport's midnight bustle and noise overwhelmed them. They had never seen so many people, all hurrying somewhere – but they found Sione's uncle Semi exactly where he said he would be and quickly followed him to his car.

The boys' eyes were as big as clamshells, watching the streaming traffic stretching away forever into the night. Mele, happy and undaunted by the exciting new world swirling around her just smiled while Sione wondered if they were doing the right thing bringing their small family to this awesome madhouse.

Semi practiced in Otara as a lawyer, mainly handling conveyancing deals and disputes rather than criminal cases. He had done well over the years, and owned a large home in nearby East Tamaki with plenty of space for the new arrivals.

He had happily given his time, advice and money to help other Tongans – especially family – improve their own life-styles.

Within a week, the new arrivals had settled into suburban South Auckland, the wider city's Polynesian enclave with its predominantly clean and neat state house style homes, clipped lawns and gardens that displayed lemon trees and flax rather than coconut palms and hibiscus.

A civic pride had grown with schools, sports grounds, churches, health centres and other public amenities but Otara's small and grubby town centre was a blot with its untidy rows of shops, takeaway food outlets and the Paradise Bar and Pokies Sione knew he would never visit.

Through his many business contacts, Semi arranged a job for Sione in an Otara warehouse filling orders, re-stocking, stacking and, once he knew his way around, making deliveries. The position was basic by Auckland standards but offered many extra overtime hours so he was paid well compared with his pittance at home – the boat seemed closer already.

Sione liked the warehouse work and his fellow workers, while Mele got a cleaning job at the local hospital and seemed happy all the time – especially at home where, for the first time in her life, she had electric power at the flick of a switch for lighting and cooking, hot and cold running water from an indoor tap, a television set in Semi's lounge and buses which ran on time to the biggest city she had ever seen.

In Auckland, a 30-minute bus ride away, she spent hours walking and looking at the towers touching the sky, shop windows crammed with goods and clothing she had never even dreamed of at home, ferry boats crossing the wide harbour, the huge bridge, and, strangely, the white people who looked so unhappy to be part of this wildly exciting place.

The boys were enrolled in a nearby secondary school, did well at their classes and - fast, fit and with the promise of their father's strong physique – made the under-17 rugby team, playing furiously alongside their palagi, Samoan, Maori and other Tongan mates.

They soon had newspaper delivery rounds, earning enough money to see a movie, unheard of in Nuku'alofa, when they were not playing sport, studying or going to church.

Sione watched his savings account grow as the months passed quickly but increasingly he felt the three people he loved most dearly were growing distant and somehow following a path quite separate from his own.

Everything should have been perfect but he could not ignore a nagging unease at how quickly and comfortably Mele and the boys had embraced their new lives far from the islands. They seemed not to miss the warmth, the flowers, their close family, the Tongan way – and their Mother Ocean.

He discussed his concerns with his Tongan workmates before they left for the Paradise when their shifts ended but they just laughed and advised him to enjoy the money, the city, the good times – and to buy a coat if he was cold.

His depression deepened, made worse when Mele came home one day wearing a smart palagi-style frock and stole. She had bought the garments not from the glistening downtown stores but at the local Red Cross and Hospice op-shops for just a few dollars but the effect was the same.

He saw how quickly she had become immersed in her new lifestyle far from Ha'apai and Nuku'alofa. She now had new friends, independence, modern conveniences, cinemas, an exciting city and even corner stores that sold more than basic goods.

She too wanted a better life but it was here in South Auckland rather than the Kingdom's poverty and archaic social restrictions.

Like his warehouse friends, Mele and the boys were here to stay. Their memories of home with its pretty islands and flowers would fade – and he as a faithful husband could not desert them despite the despair eating into his bones.

Sione sat on the front steps of Semi's fine house, watching a cold rain shower creep along the street – and dreamed of boats.

NEW TALES OF THE SOUTH PACIFIC
Volume 2: No place for dreamers

Tale 3   CANE

It is hard country up there in the Vitogo foothills behind Lautoka: hard, hot – and very dry.

There has been no rain for a long time and the sugar cane is topped with mauve-grey feathery plumes as the vast untended crops flower above the dry red soil.

Cane is seldom seen in flower. The crop is usually cut and sent to the mills at Ba, Rakiraki, Labasa and Lautoka for crushing to extract its sweet syrupy sap months before the soft colour appears.

But this year, hundreds of acres are withering, drying in the ground and the Indian growers are refusing to harvest, instead allowing the rich sap to nourish the seeds developing within the flower-heads – the cane becomes less valuable as every searing day passes and they know there will be no cash return from the past year of crippling toil.

The Fiji Indian cane farmers are among the Pacific's poorest people but have chosen to watch their wives and children starve with them rather than bring in the cutting gangs after the first of Colonel Sitiveni Rabuka's two 1987 military coups which ended the democratically elected but Indian-majority government of Timoce Bavadra.

Rabuka was the front man for Fiji's indigenous Melanesians, the Taukei, who believed they were losing their country to "outsiders." They felt threatened and "Fiji for Fijians" became the battle cry as Rabuka and his lieutenants marched into the Suva parliament and ended Bavadra's short but popular moment in the sun.

Indian homes and businesses were stoned, foreign media who rushed in to cover the event were jostled and those who disapproved of the Pacific's first black dictator were intimidated.

There was less protest and outrage from Fiji's closest neighbours than there would have been to an outbreak of herpes at Lucky Eddie's – just another hiccup from those people in the islands, they said, and it would soon go away.

But the Indians did care – especially those in the hard, hot and dry Vitogo foothills.

They put their pride and willingness to accept terrible hardship above meek obedience to the Colonel who would become known as Steve Rambo, and allow their crops to wither in a show of defiance well organised by the farmers' union, the powerful Kissan Sangh.

They are men as hard as the land they work, living barely above the poverty line, earning perhaps NZ$1500 for a year's back-breaking effort.

We sip yaqona in the sparse shade of a spreading rain tree at Qalitu and it is a welcome rest after the hot, dusty and jarring drive on the long rock-dirt road from Lautoka to Karen Singh's small leased property.

Kissan Sangh organisers, Dhani and Jay Raj, have called a meeting of Vitogo district farmers to update them on Rabuka's latest rants from Suva and discuss new strategies that might help the cause of these men whose families have worked this land for three or more generations.

They know the union would have their crops burned at night if they weaken, would call in the cutting gangs and then sell their harvest to the mills.

Rabuka, too, knows that fires would come in the darkness if he ordered his soldiers to cut the cane to bring in desperately needed export dollars.

The farmers' sari-clad wives and round-eyed children stare at their husbands and fathers from behind Singh's few pitiful huts that serve as his family home and try not to think of food –

they share what little they have but hunger is never far away.

The hard Indian men joke that the 10 of us would all be thrown in gaol if a patrol drove up the road – Rabuka had banned gatherings of more than three people – so that even a gang of cane cutters would be illegal.

We all laugh in the still shade above the mauve-topped miles of drying cane painting the landscape toward the Pacific with the Yasawas sprinkled like jewels on the horizon – while along the coast below, Fijian waiters run drinks to American, New Zealand and Australian tourists lounging poolside at the resorts.

Ram Bernard, a black hawk of a man who has known nothing in his life but hard labour, tells us that he and his family must care for his widowed sister-in-law and her two sons and daughter on his small farm at Buabua, further down the Vitogo Valley – they have no one else.

"We will suffer very much," he says. "We rely on cane for everything. There is no other income and we will have to plant other crops like dab (duruka, or Fiji asparagus) to survive.

"The only weapon we have is refusing to cut the cane. We do not have guns, we cannot march in protest. Now is the time to make a stand and we must finish it. This way we are hurting them the hardest. We will burn the cane ourselves if the army tries to cut it."

Ram has farmed here all his life and with his wife and four children scratches out a bare existence from his tiny holding, living on meals of rice and dahl and curried-anything with rhoti – an Indian pancake made from a coarse brown flour called sharp.

"There will be no harvest this year," he says, gazing silently under the hard, hot sky across the mauve flower carpet to the sea.

Karen Singh, like almost all the Vitogo growers and thousands who went before them, is inured to hardship.

Fiji's British colonists in the mid-1800s realised the economic potential of sugar as a replacement for copra as the islands' main export commodity crop, but did not want to risk upsetting the traditional Fijian way of life by putting Taukei into the cane fields – and they shunned the cruel blackbirding trade which forcibly imported other Pacific islanders as slaves.

Instead, their solution was to bring in more than 62,000 Indians as indentured labour from their homelands – mainly from the Punjab and Gujarat provinces – from 1879 until 1916. Only a third returned to India when their contracts expired, as most planned a fine new life in the tropical Pacific.

Many stayed with sugar cane while others aspired to greater roles as businessmen, doctors, lawyers, traders – and politicians – in the new society they were helping to shape.

"It will be very bad for us this year without the cane," Karen Singh says. "But that is a better thing than cutting and seeing the money go to the army."

The dark, determined faces under the raintree slowly nod agreement and a final bilo of yaqona is passed around as we farewell our hosts before the long hot and dusty drive through the flowering cane back to Lautoka.

Unlike the almost-penniless cane growers, thousands of professional and wealthier Fiji Indians left the islands forever after the two Rabuka coups and the subsequent power grabs by businessman George Speight and Commodore Frank Bainimarama.

The naval officer, confronted with political issues and disagreements with the high chiefs, in 2006 took the position of Prime Minister –

prompting the media to refer to Fiji as a "Bainimarama Republic."

This time, the international community reacted to the civil rights abuse with embargoes and travel bans, although tourists, mostly from New Zealand and Australia, continued to put economy before morality, and lured by cheap packages, flocked to the beaches and lagoons.

Fiji Indians numbered around 314,600 – 37.6 percent of the total population — at the 2007 census – and some sort of ragged cohabitation exists even after so many years without a true democracy in the islands. They are the sugar industry, vital to whoever holds the power – legally or not – and its huge economic benefits would be crippled without them.

The Fiji Sugar Corporation, headed by an Indian executive chairman, recently announced vastly improved production and expected export earnings of at least F$30 million for 2011.

The Vitogo foothills are still a hard, hot place to toil, but Karen Singh and his neighbours work as they always have done – and get on with their lives in the harsh landscape as they have always done.

The Kissan Sangh still visits to sip yaqona under the rain tree and discuss events in the capital and – here in the cane belt – the crops, the weather, market prices, families and anything except the black year when the mauve flower carpet stretched to the sea.

NEW TALES OF THE SOUTH PACIFIC
Volume 2: No place for dreamers

Tale 4 THE LAST RESORT

The room smelled of death. A rotten black kind of death even the sad-eyed, dangle-eared, loopy pup at Jack's bedside seemed to sense.

The hibiscus-patterned red curtains were drawn to block the bright sunlight so that the low table and its cigarette packet, empty Vailima bottle and spilled glass loomed in the hot, stinking humidity of the place.

It's like a cell, I thought, and looked down at its prisoner.

Jack's skin was whiter than the sand of the lagoon not far from the door, his face streaked and beaded with an oily exudation that was more than sweat, his hair stringy and long matted to his forehead. He was gazing at me, darkened pupils ringed white and the lids carrying little loads of whatever gummed them tight when he slept, which I presumed was most of the time now.

The filthy grey sheet was blotched with the poisons and bile he dribbled since the sickness took him.

"It's good to see you," he whispered, raising himself with difficulty onto an elbow and reaching for a cigarette.

"Thought I'd drop in and see how you're doing. It's been a long while Jack."

I watched as he dragged on the cigarette and waited for the explosion of coughing and gagging, but it didn't come.

"Yeah, that it has old buddy. They were good days then – we had a lot of laughs."

"We sure did. But how's it going over here? How's the place doing?"

"Oh, just great." He stubbed the hardly touched cigarette into the ashtray. "It's a bit quiet right now, but we're usually pretty full with tourists. They've started coming here in droves, mate – Jack's Place is really catching on with the diving, sailing and just lying around with a cold Vailima. It's a great spot."

Jack's eyes glinted with some of the old fire, as they did when his rugby team was one point ahead with two minutes left on the clock. Like they did when he introduced us to the girl he had flown up from New Zealand to marry.

It was his second and her first and she was enraptured by his tales of his special place in the South Pacific – the beauty, the easy living and, yes, Paradise.

He had left an accounting job in town and bought a major share in this little resort across the island on the south coast, a fine place with a deep jungled river flowing into the north end of a clear coral lagoon with the reef's thunder a mile out into the endless ocean.

That was two years ago and neither the marriage nor the resort had ever been a success. They both knew that.

Visitors saw the peeling paint on the buildings, sat down to a lunch of curried sausages, stayed a night on the lumpy, sagging beds in the crack-walled, nothing-worked guest rooms and soon left to tell their friends not to bother with the place over the hill run by the young-old sick man.

Jack lit another cigarette and gazed at the empty Vailima bottle. "Got a couple more in the fridge, mate – you'll find a glass in the kitchen. You'll have to rinse it though."

Jack kept talking while I got the beers. I drank from the bottle.

"Yeah, we had record figures both years. They love this place. You should have been here last week – we had a terrific mob of Australians staying and the bar didn't shut. We drank and danced and screwed till dawn." He tried to laugh but choked on the beer and smoke. "It was real good," he managed to gasp.

I didn't ask about the plump blonde Jack had brought from New Zealand to be his wife. She was a pleasant girl, I remembered, who kept him happy enough for a while and life, for the first time in many years, began to look good for my old friend.

But like so many others who had come to these islands with preconceived ideas of Paradise, her new life soon paled. She wanted two television channels when none existed, stores fully stocked to cater for every whim, telephones that worked, buses that ran on time and European friends to talk with about babies, knitting and husbands.

Then on a fine, hot June day, she had taken a cab to Faleolo and flown back to Papatoetoe or Porirua or whatever featureless suburb she had come from – and who could blame her?

She hadn't even left a note for Jack, but he understood and never tried to contact her.

He stayed on, dreaming of the days soon when he would be turning tourists away from this lovely place, when they came and laughed and loved the lagoon and the little hotel, the big river, the sweet flowers and jungled hills sweeping down to the white sand and far-off reef. That was the dream keeping him alive – and he believed it.

"Since they started coming, you know, I've had a couple of big international hotel chains and an airline or two interested in taking over – and they're talking big money. They can see what I've got going here and they want a piece of it. Just think, with investment like that we can start thinking about tennis courts, a golf course, swimming pool . . . another block of rooms at the top end of the lagoon.

"It's all about to happen, mate."

I got two more beers and poured Jack's for him. He was looking better, energised by his talk of the dream, the offshore cash and a resort to rival the Pacific's best. The pup rested its muzzle on the dirty bedsheet, sighed heavily and closed its sad eyes – He'd heard it all before.

"This is all I've always wanted, mate. The airport up-grade will be finished soon and there won't be enough beds in the country to handle all the tourists. This is really going so be something. You should see the plans we've got to expand this place – my lawyer in town has got them so give him a call and tell him I said you could look at them. You'll be bloody impressed, I know.

"The government is flat broke and they know tourism will bring in millions so the next step will be a casino – imagine that, a casino right here on my beach. The big spenders will come flocking in. I'll get the best chefs, world-class acts, dance bands, perhaps a disco for the youngies, a couple of charter boats for big-game fishing . . ."

Jack fell backward on the bed, coughing and gagging and spilling his beer over the startled pup. He lay back exhausted on the filthy pillow in the dark room that smelled of death, panting, fighting for breath, trembling with his eyes closed and his face awash with a new coat of oily sweat.

He whispered hoarsely, so soft I could barely hear his voice. "I'll try and get down to the bar and buy you a beer. Twenty minutes?"

Outside, the air was alive with tradewind sunshine, the palms nodding and shuffling, the reef surf a thundering ragged white strip way out against the deep blue ocean and the lagoon clear and crisp beyond the clean white sand beach.

I swam out fifty yards, splashing diamonds in the salt-sun and wondered how long it had been since Jack had dived and laughed and watched the whites, pinks, reds and golds of fish and coral slide beneath him. How long since he had grinned with the sheer joy of sun on his face, shaken water from his hair and run up the beach and across the coarse thick grass under the palms to the Lagoon Bar and laughed again with the pleasure of an ice-cold Vailima bubbling down his throat.

Cruising slowly back to the shore through the warm clear water, distance veils the resort's rundown appearance and Jack's Place is a neat, functional single-storey row of buildings and fales sprinkled with hibiscus and frangipani – tiny below the green peaks that are the island's spine.

I imagine where the tennis courts might be built, the pool, disco, casino and, at the top end of the beach, new accommodation blocks. The top end is a swamp.

The steady warm suck of the trades caresses sensuously through the Lagoon Bar where the laughing-eyed island girl is happy to have a customer. She pours a glass of draught beer and chatters merrily about her brothers and sisters back in their village on Savai'i, the big island.

She says she is the lucky one of the family, escaping the strictness of family and matai when she moved to the bright lights of Apia to work as one of the many girls at the legendary Aggie Grey's Hotel.

That had been a wonderful experience, but here she is Number One girl – chief house-keeper, barmaid, meeter, greeter, check-in, check-out, room service, gear hire, problem-fixer and after-midnight anything-you-wanter. It's a great job.

But it would be even greater if a tourist or two would drive down the spectacular jungle road from town and stay even for just a few days. Just a few would make a big difference and she sometimes despairs of the loneliness, the emptiness, the decay and death.

So does Jack.

His twenty minutes is long past and I finish a third beer, farewell the ever-hopeful barmaid and walk in the sun with the warm trades to Jack's room. Inside, it is still dark and hot and still stinks. The pup's head is slumped on its paws and its eyes are shut although the tail makes a couple of tired sweeps as I enter – just for the record.

Jack's eyes are glued shut and he has turned to face the wall.

"Is that you, mate?"

I sit beside him on the bed and notice he has put on a clean shirt. "I tried to make the bar, mate, I really did."

He doesn't move. Only his voice, slow and softly whispered, tells me there is life in this once-laughing, rugby playing lover of all things vibrant, exciting and new. I place a hand on his agonisingly thin shoulder but he doesn't move.

"Do you want to tell me what's wrong, Jack?"

He groans softly and the sound becomes the saddest I have ever heard. "I'm buggered if I know, mate. I'm buggered if I know."

Later that night at Aggie's I nurse my fifth double and cannot cleanse myself of death and the worst kind of loneliness.

NEW TALES OF THE SOUTH PACIFIC
Volume 2: No place for dreamers

Tale 5 PALAGIS AT PLAY

We are out by the pool beside the big fale under a million stars thrown across the velvet night and everyone is drinking far too much good Australian burgundy at a table that has death wish stamped all over it.

The bad jokes and drunken laughter are getting louder, shattering the tropical calm in a way which marks expatriates the world over.

Big Rod is leading the push and Jimmy the Joint is trying successfully to make out with a pipe-smoking blonde German divorcee while Helen's face keeps slipping into her glass. Young Williams doesn't do this sort of thing often on his salary and he ignores his porcelain wife whose glares carry the single unmistakable message that he's too drunk, too loud and sex is definitely off for at least a week.

Williams, an insurance clerk on a short island posting from his Dunedin head office, is laughing at every joke whether he understands them or not and openly admiring the lithe brown waitresses gliding past, yearning desperately to just touch one to see if they are real, and if so, take her home for a pet.

Mrs. Williams, though, yearns only for the familiarity and comfort of the southern city where she was born, grew up and had no desire to ever leave, with or without her undemanding and conscientious husband who was always so soberly predictable.

Life on the island is unbearable for her. The heat is stifling, the lagoons are probably alive with woman-eating sharks, the village singing is too loud, the food is inedible and she doesn't trust her house-girl or the cockroaches.

She is disgusted and very angry at the scene she has unwillingly become part of but no one gives a damn except the 300-or-so after-dinner tourists wearied after a day's sight-seeing from the back of a jolting bus and now squashed together in the fale only feet away to watch an old big-screen James Bond movie on this warm black night under the palms by the pool.

Tempted by the tourist brochures' Paradise promises, they have paid package tour prices to come to the island and taste the tropics, the gentle people, the lagoons and reefs. They are not impressed by Rod ending a grubby action story about a moustached and sweating Tongan he assumed was female who enthusiastically took part in an unnatural sexual encounter out the back of Joe's Bar last time he was in Nuku'alofa and the fight that followed when he refused to pay, telling her to piss off because she seemed to have enjoyed it more than he did.

The table explodes in a cacophony of shrieks and screams of mock horror, another empty bottle smashes onto the concrete and the nearest 100 Bond fans glare from the fale as Sean Connery flounders in a sea of pink satin before going down for the third time.

77

The German divorcee asks the Joint, "Vott voss he telling about?" The Joint tries to show her right there at the table, but suggests instead that they adjourn to her nearby room for enlightenment.

Rod and the Joint – so named for the suspicious soggy roll-your-own usually seen dangling from the side of his mouth – are hard players, expatriates and good friends well-respected by the islanders who often work for them in their construction businesses.

They are from similar working class backgrounds, coming to the islands to escape the cities, the crowds, the cons and wives grown bored and cold.

Rod, a builder, and The Joint, a concreter, often work together on big contracts. Both are popular employers for the way they treat their gangs, on the job and socially – both men share bonuses with their workers and crack a box or two of Vailima after work on Friday nights.

Here they have found their own brand of basic Nirvana with plenty of humour shared with island friends, swimming and diving in the magic lagoons, great local food and beer and good, honest work – especially after the devastating cyclone seasons.

Unlike some expats who come to the islands wearing their obvious European breeding like high-rank epaulettes that signal superiority and who are never seen mingling with the native people, they have learned more than the basics of the local language, deepening the high degree of respect in which they are held.

Neither have plans to leave the island, although both realise that the day will eventually come – for whatever reason – when they will have to move on. Nowhere does Nirvana last forever.

Bryan, the new bank manager, tries to avoid the glares from the sea of movie-watchers as he makes his way to the bar for another round of drinks no one really needs. His wife Helen slops more red down her copious cleavage and lurches for the table.

"Oh, shit," she slurs. "I must be getting a bit over the limit – but what else do you expect? What else is there to do in this dump, but go out and party and get pissed? I wish I was back in Wellington, it's so much nicer there and at least you can get what you want in the super-market.

"You know, they were out of toilet rolls here last week – can you imagine that? Thank God Bryan is someone important, he's with the bank you know, so at least we do meet some other important people. At least we do get to some decent cocktail parties with some decent people.

"They didn't have any New Zealand cheese today and we haven't seen Wattie's baked beans for over a week. I've had to get by on some terrible American gunk from Pago or somewhere.

"I can't imagine what this is doing to the children's education – they haven't seen any of their favourite TV shows for more than a year except when they go home and sit in front of the screen for hours to try and catch up.

"And what makes this place even worse is that I can't understand what the natives are saying – they could be saying the most awful things about me and how would I know? I've tried shouting at them to make them understand what I want, but they just smile and walk away giggling – it's infuriating.

"Thank God, Bryan is up here for only three years. I really can't stand it much longer – there's absolutely nothing to do. I already play bridge with the girls four days a week to stop myself going mad. New Zealand butter is late again this week. I wish I could play bridge seven days a week."

The monologue was largely unheard. Williams and his porcelain wife were arguing; The Joint and the divorcee had adjourned to her room; and Rod had wandered off to the toilet, either to take a leak or throw up.

He doesn't return and I know how he feels. I, too, could walk out on these pitiful palagis, but my masochistic streak forces me to stay for the finale of this sad, mad tableau.

Bryan is back with more burgundy and watches expressionless at his wife's outpourings of nothing, one hand thrusting her empty glass at no one in particular, the other caressing the thigh nearest hers.

Wine dribbles down his chin and he can only stare at his wife, now gripping more firmly, more intimately with the unmistakable message that – "yes, it is on, if only I can get rid of this wimp of a husband of mine.

She attempts to combine a seductive sidelong wink with a long sip from the refilled wineglass and predictably slops more burgundy down her breasts. She giggles and returns her husband's stare while slipping her neighbour's hand under her hemline.

He closes his eyes and I think he is going to cry, but I don't know if the tears would be for his drunk wife or the boardroom in Wellington. Ah, Bryan – you should know by now that booze and sex are the great South Pacific panacea for pale people who don't colour in the sun.

A late night trade sets the palm fronds whispering and the pool surface shimmers at its passing. Across Upolu, I know fishermen will be out on the reef with their lanterns and the eternal crashing surf will be pounding Lefaga's basalt ramparts. The fales in the villages along the beach road to Faleolo will be quiet under the palms, and perhaps a tropic moon is bathing Stevenson's tomb on Mt Vaea's green peak.

The movie is over and the disgruntled audience drifts away. The table by the pool is wine-slopped and empty now and the fale bar is closed, but Helen demands more drink despite Bryan's pleas that she call it a night and come home with him. She lurches away from his offered helping hand and, inevitably, falls into the pool – to the merriment of a dozen hotel cleaners.

Christ! I hope Otto's is still open.

NEW TALES OF THE SOUTH PACIFIC
Volume 2: No place for dreamers

Tale 6 THE ENDS

"I have come here to die," the Scottish novelist Robert Louis Stevenson wrote home to a friend, "and if you care to visit, you will find it a fine place for the purpose."

Susan and David, basking by the pool at Aggie Grey's Hotel almost in the shadow of Mt Vaea which provides a startling backdrop to Apia, Samoa's capital and the South Pacific's most romantic, historic, laid-back and insane port town, had probably never heard those words from the great Tusitala whose body rests in a white tomb atop the jungled peak.

But they shared a common goal with the classic author, for they had also come here to die.

Old, trusted and platonic friends who had often visited Samoa with their spouses, they had also been to the island as a twosome — partied, adventured, laughed and lived the Fa'a Samoa way and made many friends in the town, villages, nightclubs and bars around Apia. They were well-known and well-liked by the happy locals and the respect was mutual.

But Susan in the past few days had begun to question their decision to let it all end in their one particular harbour, perhaps worrying about the gossip, the accusations from friends a world away in Auckland.

"Are you still sure this is the right thing to do?" she asked, pleading into David's face. "I mean, other people just don't do it this way. They go to hospital or a hospice and have a proper funeral in a church with all their family and friends — they don't just disappear and go partying. Well, do they?"

David drank deeply from his cold bottle of Vailima and moved out of the umbrella shade to work on his tan again. He lit another cigarette and blew smoke in a long stream toward the sparkling pool.

He sighed. Susan's eyes had not left his face. "Well, do they?" she insisted.

"No they don't, and that's probably because everyone is so hung up about death. You know we're not the types to hang around and get sicker and skinnier and sadder and weaker in front of our families until we die a miserable death in a dark room with them all standing around sobbing. "Come on Susan, you know that's not for us."

"Yes I know all that, but this is really weird. We're supposed to be on our way out – dying – but they all know we're up here having a good time."

"Hey, let's not get into this again. We made the decision, agreed it was our way of dealing with our terminal issue Susan so let's get on with it. Come on, it's your turn to go to the bar, but go easy on the rum – you know what it's doing to your liver."

"Sure," Susan threw a piece of ice at him, "and smoking will kill you." She laughed brightly and skipped toward the thatched pool bar. David knew another moment of doubt had passed, that it was all right again.

It had been a terrible shock, of course, and David had retreated into himself like a crippled thing afraid to face the whole and healthy ones. He hadn't bothered going to the office again, just phoned and told them he'd resigned and to put his severance cheque in the mail and clear his desk.

David was staring at death and it would not go away. "I am terribly sorry, David," his doctor had told him one blustery March day. "The results of the tests are very bad news. I have taken advice and opinions from the best specialists, and they agree there is nothing more to be done . . . ."

"Let's not piss around Richard, how long have I got?"

"Four months at the most. This is a condition which can be forecast very accurately."

"Jesus," he breathed, "just four bloody months?"

David only half-listened to his doctor explain that there would be little discomfort right to the end that the virus had invaded his brain and the invasion would continue until one day soon he would, quite simply, cease to function. He would stop living, which, he mused, was probably a nicer way of saying dying.

He recalled seeing his doctor a year ago after his sight on two or three occasions faded to a blur and he had bouts of deafness. They would clear after 15 or 20 minutes and he tried not to move too far in an effort to keep his composure so that others did not notice his distress. He bluffed his way through those awful times but in the end, that tiny little virus was winning.

After two weeks of moping, drinking too much vodka, making excuses for not keeping engagements, and hanging up on his vacuous ex-wife Joan, David decided to do something with what little was left of his life.

He gave the cat to neighbours, telling them he was going on a long journey, and then set about saying farewells to the few really close friends he had. Among them were Susan and John, a lively professional couple who regularly made a foursome before he and Joan split. They remained good friends, understanding each other's strengths and weaknesses, laughing at the same dumb jokes and exhilarating experiences – especially on the island where they had often holidayed and partied together.

David had twice vacationed with Susan when business pressures prevented John from joining them. They were secure in each other's company and no one ever doubted their relationship was anything but platonic.

Susan poured a large rum with a little Coke and swallowed it in a gulp. Her eyes watered and she almost gagged with the shock of it. Sitting in the big chair by the window, staring out over the lawns and garden wearing its autumn tints, she began to cry. Susan wept silently, not bothering to wipe away the tears trickling through her make-up. She was a fine-looking woman who at 45 had that long chestnut hair and a figure that still turned men's heads.

She knew she was beautiful and she was proud of the gift. She was also proud of John and their 25-year marriage and two daughters, but now she was so afraid because all she honoured would soon vanish very quickly and very horribly.

"The treatment sounds harsh I know and the success rate is only 20 percent," Dr. Foster told her. "But there is a chance. You will suffer weight loss, there will be long periods of nausea and, yes, I'm afraid there will have to be mastectomies. Chemotherapy has been used very successfully for many years, Susan, and I urge you to have this treatment. The alternative is, well, I can promise you no more than four months."

Susan carried the beer and rum back to the poolside table under the soaring coconut palms in time to see David ogling a long-legged blonde nymphet stretching like a cat on her towel under the frangipani.

"Don't you ever give up?" she laughed.

"Never. Everyone you miss is one you'll never get," he grinned, white teeth startling white against his tan.

"Well you'd better hurry. We're running out of time."

"Hey," he grimaced, "that hurt."

"No, stupid. I wasn't making a crack about our, um, situation. It's nearly four and if we're going to meet the guys at the Reef, we'd better start moving.

He grinned. "You drink too much."

"Piss off," she said, and dived into the pool.

It had been easier than they had imagined. Kindred spirits, David and Susan had taken converging paths that quickly met at a concurrent point to decide their short futures. After the initial shocking realisation that they had somehow been given identical sentences, they became united in refusing to sit and wait for death, to wither and droop in an ocean of increasingly dark sadness.

They could never recall who first suggested returning to the island, to sun and party, feast and drink, swim and paddle in the warm lagoons under the endless sun with the thunder of the reef half a mile out, to laugh and sing under the tumbling waterfalls dropping like silver through the green and flowered jungles of the high country.

Nor could they recall which of them had first shrugged off the blackness of despair and begun to enthuse about a final holiday, one glorious fling with old island friends, the ultimate bucket-list item — a reckless celebration of life while laughing in the face of death as it crept irresistibly closer as each hour passed. It was a freakish opportunity neither could resist and after all, it was their call.

A sudden drenching downpour had sprung out of the mountains and swept across the little town before marching across the lagoon and out to sea leaving the air steaming inside the dark, hot and noisy little beachfront bar.

"Hi Frankie, Louisa," David shouted above Jimmy Buffett and the Coral Reefers thundering at a thousand decibels from the stereo speakers under the leaking iron roof. Louisa turned from pulling draft Vailima for a group of laughing locals and flashed her wide Samoan smile.

Frankie was already pouring their usuals, a huge vodka-tonic for David and Susan's rum and Coke.

"Hi guys," the bartender slid their glasses across the bar. "Another shitty day in Paradise?"

"Someone's got to do it," Susan laughed. "I've even stopped wondering what the poor people are doing."

"I envy you guys," Frankie said. "You've been up here, what, nearly two months this time and you're getting so much sun you're darker than I am. How long are you staying?"

"As long as it takes," David murmured. "As long as it bloody takes."

"Hey, we aren't getting the gloomies are we?" Susan asked as the barman moved away to serve another group of locals. "Not after your little lecture to me today."

"No, not at all. I just realised that it has been two months and I started to wonder about the next two or whatever. We've never really talked about what happens when we really start to, er, deteriorate. We've concentrated only on the upside, which of course was the whole idea, but I'm starting to think about the big downer to come."

"Well you'd better stop thinking that way – here comes the team."

A half-dozen couples made Friday nights a regular party together, meeting at the Reef for rounds of drinks and later eating at one of Apia's many small cafes before drinking and dancing past midnight at the packed and sweating backstreet clubs in the little harbour town.

They drank, they laughed, they talked and joked and above the stereo thunder tried to focus on their reasons for being here. It was an ideal environment for David, whose waves of deafness and veiled vision went unnoticed in the crowded cacophony. Susan, shielded by drugs from the gnawing pain inside her, could have been a teenager on her first date, David thought. Tonight she glowed and sparkled. She was very alive.

Later they ate shrimp at the Sunrise, a little café built on spindly posts over the water behind the markets, and drank ice-cold San Miguel until, fortified; they ended the night with a round of the clubs and discos. It was past three a.m. when friends dropped them unsteadily back at Aggie's, and for the first time, he went to her room.

David woke late with the mist over his eyes. He could not see but knew he was alone in the bed and felt the awful guilt. He lay still until his vision returned, then dressed and walked quickly to his room, hoping he would not be seen by the armies of housegirls who thrived on gossip.

Showered and dressed in clean clothes, he was choking his way through a first cigarette and coffee by the pool when she walked slowly up to him. Her sad smile said it all.

"God, Susan, I'm so sorry. What can I say?"

"Please don't David. It takes two, you know."

"But that wasn't supposed to happen. It wasn't ever like that. I'm so damned sorry." He saw then that she was wearing the pink shirt and white frilled blouse she wore on the flight from Auckland and he knew she was leaving. Behind her, a porter wheeled her suitcase on a trolley toward reception.

She caught his glance and placed a hand gently on his shoulder. "Don't blame yourself, David. It was my decision too; but it is also my decision now to go home to John. It's been a wonderful two months here and I think we achieved what we set out to do – but now it's time."

Susan leaned forward, kissed him lightly on the forehead then turned and walked away without looking back. The hotel bus was leaving for the airport. David watched her go and felt an overwhelming loneliness. His eyes were misty as he walked to the bar and ordered a large vodka – but this time he knew it was not the virus.

David drove slowly on the cross-island road climbing out of the town, clinging to the lower slopes then on into the higher country to leave the heat and humidity of the coast. He passed Vailima where Stevenson had died at 44 almost a century ago and glanced up at Mt Vaea's peak where the writer's tomb with a bronze plaque bearing a Scottish thistle and Samoan hibiscus forever frame his unforgettable epitaph:

> *Here he lies where he longed to be.*
> *Home is the sailor, home from sea,*
> *And the hunter home from the hill.*

He crawled on, stopping briefly at the Tiave Falls to allow another wave of mist and deafness to pass before descending to the breathtaking first sight of the scalloped lagoons and reefs of the south coast.

David parked the car in a coconut grove at Tafa Tafa beach, a special place he and Susan had loved and visited many times to swim in its wide lagoon, picnic on its long sweep of white sand and listen to the thunder of the reef. They had paddled outrigger canoes and marvelled at the ocean's power as the great rollers crashed and surged and thundered on the coral ramparts, aware of the dangers that lay in the deepest of waters beyond.

He dragged an outrigger off the beach and began paddling through water so clear he could see every grain of sand on the bottom, stroking effortlessly across the breeze-rippled surface to glide smoothly toward the reef.

He understood perfectly why Susan had returned home. It had been a wonderfully mad plan, but she was right — they had achieved all they had set out to do, to look death in the face and laugh until it came too close to ignore any longer.

The warm trade wind increased half a mile from shore, whipping ripples into wavelets that slopped and splashed as he drove the paddle harder and faster into the water. He felt wonderful; the sun on his back, his muscles working in perfect rhythm on this picture-book lagoon gave him an exhilarating sense of complete freedom, release, escape.

David changed course slightly to line up with the gap in the reef where white water surged and roared in an eternal explosion of thunder. The mists returned to blind him as he paddled fast and strong for the gap. He was in a silent world of movement and beauty and did not see the salt spray from his paddle sparkling like handfuls of diamonds in the sun, nor the deep blue of the deepest of oceans beyond the huge

Pacific wave-mountains smashing their way into the gap.

He did not hear the screams of the seabirds working the reef above the thunder or his own voice shouting elation and triumph as the canoe flew into the roaring sea.

Available

for your Kindle reader

at Amazon.com

Visit the author's website

http://www.newtalesofthesouthpacific.com

for updates and launch date of

New Tales of the South Pacific

Volume 3

Printed in Great Britain
by Amazon

85367487R00068